CHARLES AND HIS Gee's Bend Quilt

Copyright 2021 by Tangular Irby

ALL RIGHTS RESERVED.

Published in the United States by Pen Legacy Publishing, a division of Pen Legacy, LLC, Philadelphia, PA. www.penlegacy.com

Library of Congress Cataloging – in- Publication Data has been applied for.

No part of this book may be reproduced in any written, electronic, recording, or photocopying without written permission of the publisher or author. The exception would be in the case of brief quotations embodied in the critical articles or reviews and pages where permission is specifically granted by the publisher or author.

ISBN: 978-1-7370120-9-2

PRINTED IN THE UNITED STATES OF AMERICA.

Illustrated & formatted by: India Sheana
Photography by: Olivia Ball (pink and green quilt)

First Edition

Dedication

You are the great granddaughters of Pearlie Kennedy Pettway and Jensie Lee Irby. You are the granddaughters of Florida Mae Irby and Phyllis Marin. You are heirs of a rich history that spans multiple continents. A story, yet to be told truly, that is cultivated with the blood, sweat and tears of those who came before you. May the footprints of our ancestors propel you to dream the unthinkable, guide you to your true calling and keep you in the path of your grandmother's prayers. Camille and Camryn Irby, you are my forever loves!

Always,
Your Favorite Aunt in Connecticut

On a lazy Sunday afternoon, Charles sat playing in the living room with his friends, Lucius and Robert, as the aroma of homemade biscuits, smothered chicken, rice, collard greens from the garden and grandma's famous teacakes filled the house.

"Wow, that quilt is amazing," Lucius said. "My mom has quilts like this at our house."

"Grandma told me I come from a long line of Gee's Bend quilters whose quilts have been displayed in galleries and museums all over," Charles proudly boasted. "When I get older, I'm going to make quilts too. And one of my quilts will hang over there one day." Charles pointed to the empty space where he intended to hang his work.

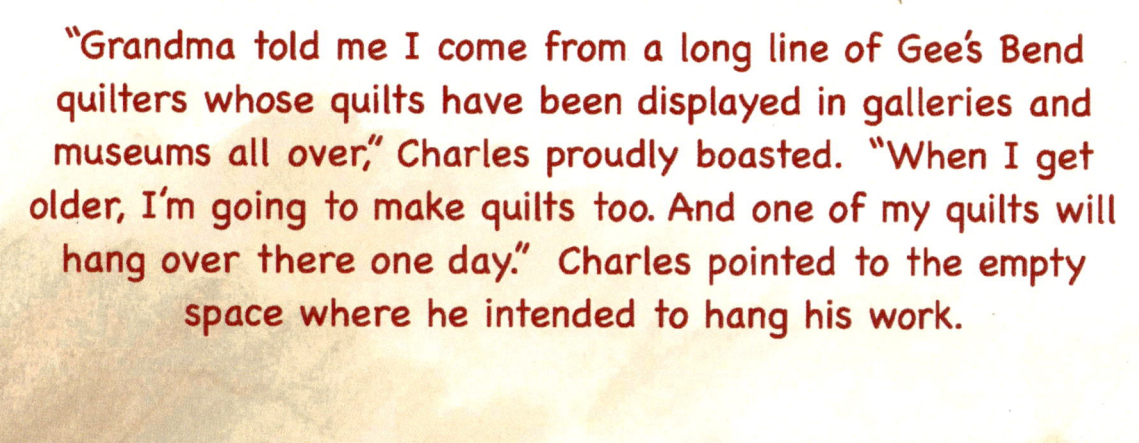

"That's pretty neat. I've never heard of that before. What are Gee's Bend quilts?," Lucius asked, wide-eyed.

Charles sat up straight, with confidence. "Back when my grandma was younger, the house she lived in did not have any heat, so she and her siblings used quilts to keep warm during winter. The families who lived in Gee's Bend, Alabama were very large. Some had ten or more children, so they needed lots of quilts.

They would tear up old clothing to use for fabric. The women would move from house to house, quilting during the evening. During the day, many of them worked at the Freedom Quilting Bee. They would use sewing machines to piece together the tops, but they quilted them together by hand."

Lucius and Robert listened in amazement, surprised that their playdate had turned into a fantastic lesson about Charles' family history.

"Grandma always says, 'Quilts are like your handwriting.'" Charles explained. "She says every quilt should be different from everyone else's. I asked Grandma how she comes up with so many different designs. She told me she talks to God when she quilts and He gives her an idea every time. I told her that I am not sure that I will be able to quilt the way she does but she told me, 'You can only do your best. You can not do my best.'"

"Helping Grandma is exciting," Charles tossed his hands in the air with a warm smile. "I get to pick the pieces of fabric that she will use next or thread the tiny needle. Sometimes, I thread 3 or 4 so they will be ready when she needs them. She even lets me fix her sewing machine when it won't work."

Lucius and Robert lay on their bellies as Charles recounted the rest of his story, his voice rising and falling like he was singing a song. "Grandma says quilting isn't always easy. Sometimes the fabric is very thick and she has to use a thimble to keep from pricking herself. One time she stuck herself and I could tell she was vexed. But no matter what, Grandma keeps quilting.

"It sounds like your grandma knows what she is doing," Robert said. I bet **YOU** can't make one!"

"Yes I can," Charles blurted in response to Robert's challenge. "Since you think you know everything, listen to this."

"The most important part of the quilt is the top. To make her special designs, Grandma sews many different scraps together. Sometimes, she uses my old clothes that don't fit anymore or grandpa's old t-shirts. Charles spoke quickly, telling everything he learned, but paused to take a breath before starting again.

"When the top is finished, the rest of the quilt is ready to be stitched together. Did you know that?"

Charles crossed his arms in satisfaction when Lucius and Robert shook their heads, then went on.

"The middle layer is called the batting. When Grandma was little, sharecroppers grew the cotton and they would pick, then flatten it for the quilts. Next comes the backing. Quilters used to use 25 lb flour sacks for the backing, but now we can go to the store to buy everything that we need."

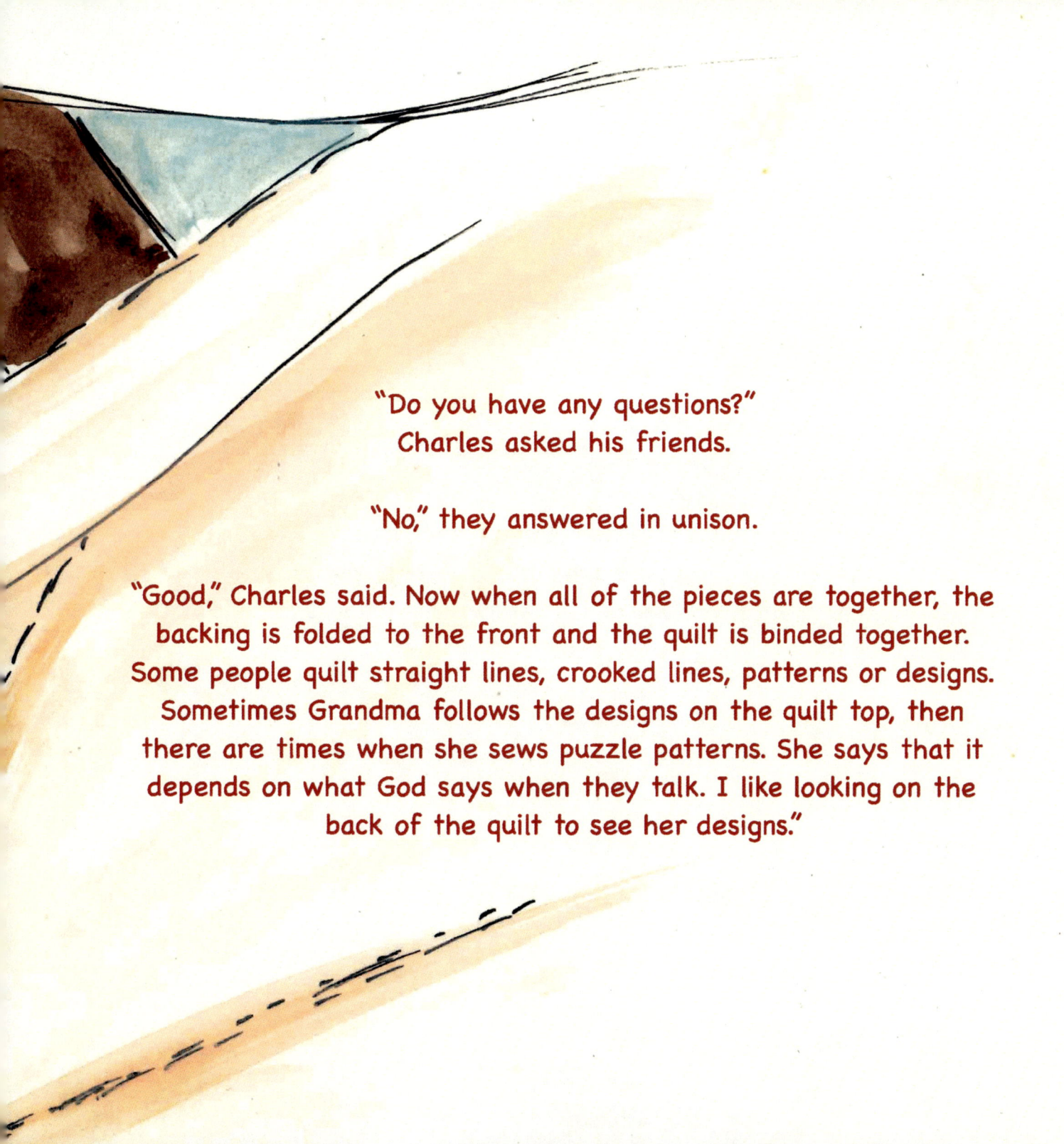

"Do you have any questions?" Charles asked his friends.

"No," they answered in unison.

"Good," Charles said. Now when all of the pieces are together, the backing is folded to the front and the quilt is binded together. Some people quilt straight lines, crooked lines, patterns or designs. Sometimes Grandma follows the designs on the quilt top, then there are times when she sews puzzle patterns. She says that it depends on what God says when they talk. I like looking on the back of the quilt to see her designs."

"Wow, Charles, you are right," Robert exclaimed. "You know a lot about quilting. Grandma says that me and my cousins need to learn so that the world will know about our quilts, too"

The boys hadn't noticed that Grandma sneaked in to eavesdrop and hear Charles teaching his friends so well. She held a few quilts in her arms as she addressed the boys with a sweet smile.

"It sounds like Charles has been watching and listening," Grandma beamed with pride. "He knows all about our family quilts and where they came from. We didn't have a lot of money back then but we always had our quilts. Our elders gave us quilts as gifts, especially when we moved up north. We got them when we married. We even got them when we came back down south for visits. Robert and Lucius, I have a gift for you. Here are your very own Gee's Bend quilts. Take good care of them."

Grandma handed each boy a quilt, and was delighted to hear them cheer with excitement. "On the back of your quilts, I have signed my name and written the name of the quilt. No one else has a quilt like yours. One day, you can pass it down to your own children and tell them the story of Gee's Bend quilts."

About the Author

Tangular A. Irby is an author, educator and quilter. She holds a BS in Business Administration, a Masters in the Art of Teaching and a 6th Year in Educational Leadership. Her love of children's books developed during her time as a second grade teacher. The power of a good book can never be overstated. She has worked professionally with all grade levels, Pre-K through 12. Most recently she has worked in higher education. She is the granddaughter of Gee's Bend quilters, Pearlie Kennedy Pettway and Jensie Lee Irby. Quilting became a way to honor their legacy.

About the Quilter

This book is based on the artistry of Mary Leatha Pettway. Born and raised in Gee's Bend, Alabama. Mary L. is a child of God, loving wife, mother and grandmother. She continues to be an active member of the small rural community. She puts God first and is not ashamed to praise him anytime or anywhere for everything he has gifted her. When she quilts she feels complete.

Visit us at www.geesbendmade.com

Made in the USA
Middletown, DE
05 January 2023